D1547982

THE CHRISTMAS WISH

A BWWM Holiday Romance

A LANGDALE CHRISTMAS
BOOK II

PEYTON BANKS

"There is only happiness in life, to love and to be loved."

— **GEORGE SAND**

Print ISBN: 978-1-956602-47-0

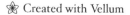 Created with Vellum

Christmas time was here and she only had one wish...

The big jolly man in the red suit was due to make his appearance in one week. Single mother Ida Dillard wanted to ensure she and her daughter Luna were ready for his arrival. She had the perfect day planned for them. It was supposed to be fun, but Mother Nature had other plans in the form of a winter snowstorm.

Local veterinarian Drew Bates was navigating the worst winter storm of the season and found a vehicle stuck in a snow drift. Being the good samaritan he was, he pulled over to help. Imagine his surprise to find it's the one woman he has been crushing on for awhile.

Drew and Ida had known each other for some time. In their cozy town of Langdale, almost everyone knew everyone. Her dog was his patient, and her best friend was married to his brother.

He ensured the girls made it home safe, but by the time they arrived, the roads were no longer drivable, and he was forced to stay the night.

With dropping temperatures and sipping hot cocoa in front of a roaring fire, the tension between the two skyrocketed. In the late night hour, all of their innocent flirting of the past went out the window. Trapped together until morning, will they seize the moment and give in to their desires?

The Christmas Wish is a steamy, holiday BWWM romance. For readers who love sexy, small town romance, this is for you. This short novella is reserved for mature readers only.

"Mom, do you think Santa will bring all the toys I asked for?" Luna asked. Ida Dillard glanced in the rearview mirror and met her young daughter's gaze. She smiled, knowing she would ensure Santa brought whatever her daughter wished for.

"Of course, he will, but that will all depend on if you have been a good girl," Ida replied.

Christmas was upon them, and it was her favorite time of the year. Every year she took her daughter to see Santa at the community center. Their small town of Langdale was nestled into the countryside of Illinois.

This was where she had grown up, and she was happy she was able to raise her daughter here.

It was a wonderful area where everyone knew everyone.

Christmas was in a week, and going to see Santa was a family tradition she had started with her daughter when they had moved to Langdale five years ago.

It was after Ida had made the hard choice to leave her husband, Clint. She tried to not think of her ex, who was a deadbeat father. Their divorce had been bitter but swift. He had given her everything she had asked for. His child support never failed to deposit into her account.

At least the son of a bitch was good for something.

But did he reach out and see to their daughter? No. Ida would be surprised if he remembered to call her on Christmas.

"I'm always a good girl, mommy." Luna's soft voice broke through Ida's thoughts. Ida smiled and had to agree with her.

"Yes, you are. Then you won't have anything to worry about." She had her daughter's Christmas list before she took it to Santa. She had priced everything and then texted Clint his half of what he owed her.

He hadn't argued. He just sent the money.

Everything her daughter wished for was already wrapped and hidden away. There was only one thing she was unable to give her daughter.

A baby sibling.

Luna had been hinting at wanting a brother or sister. She loved spending time with Gracie's son, Grayson, and insisted that they needed their own baby.

The only problem? Ida would need someone to help create a baby, and that ship had sailed a long time ago. She hadn't been sexually active in eons. There were so many cobwebs between her thighs that she was surprised she could slide her jeans through them.

"Will auntie Gracie and uncle Harris be coming to visit? I want to play with Grayson," Luna announced. "It's been forever since I've gotten to see him."

Ida smiled and tightened her grip on the

steering wheel. They had just left the community center, and the snowstorm that was promised to hit looked as if it were arriving earlier than expected.

Her best friend Gracie had finally captured the man she had been in love with since they were in high school. Harris was the perfect man for her best friend. It took them a long time to figure out they were made for each other. Anyone with eyes could see they belonged together. Once they figured it out, they did not waste time. They were married and had a son immediately.

Ida sighed. She was happy for her bestie. The only downside was Gracie had moved away from Langdale to be with Harris in Chicago.

"Yes, you know they will be here. Uncle Harris's family always has their party that we get invited to every year." Ida squinted, hating how much snow was coming down. She slowed her sedan down, feeling it begin to swerve. There must be ice on the road that she couldn't see. They didn't have far to drive, and she would hate to get stuck in this snow.

"I can't wait," Luna giggled.

"Me too. We always have fun there." Ida tried to not think of a specific person that would be there. Drew Bates, Gracie's brother-in-law, was downright gorgeous. Ida would admit she had a little crush on him. He was two years younger than her, but that didn't keep her from having fantasies about him. Drew was tall, muscular, and fit. He was also one of the town's vets and was her daughter's dog's doctor.

Even Boots, their french bulldog, was taken by Drew.

Ida was never brave enough to ask him out.

Hell, she didn't know if he even saw her. To him, she was probably Gracie's best friend and a patient's mom.

She came with baggage. Not many men wanted to date a woman with a child. She'd had a few first dates, but they never went beyond that.

Which was sad.

She and Luna made a fantastic package.

But she wasn't going to worry about that. Luna was her top priority, and getting with a man, was not.

Ida reached over and slightly turned the

radio down. Christmas songs were blaring from every station. Now she needed to concentrate. Her heart pounded as the conditions turned to nearly a whiteout.

"Mom, are we going to make it home?" Luna had pressed her face to the window. Her child had grown in the last few years. She was almost the same height as Ida. Not that was saying much. Ida was only five foot two. Clint had height to him. He was close to six feet tall. Hopefully, her daughter would get her height from her father's side.

"We are. Mommy is slowing down to make sure we don't slide off into a ditch." Ida's hands started hurting from how hard she gripped the wheel. She had grown up in Illinois and wasn't afraid of a little snow, but a storm that was different. She began thinking of what she had in the car just in case they had to pull over. There was a blanket in the trunk, and they had snacks in the car from the holiday event.

There were plenty of vendor tables to shop around for homemade gifts and snacks each year. Ida had a sweet tooth and always purchased homemade cookies. There were a few bottles of water in the car.

Hopefully, they wouldn't need to stop.

She kept her car at a steady pace and hit her hazard lights. She bit her lip and leaned forward, unable to see. Her vehicle began to pull away from her. Luna's yelp was heard as they careened off the road. She yanked the steering wheel to prevent them from sliding off the road.

But to no avail; she couldn't stop it.

Her car slammed against a snow drift.

"You okay back there?" Ida asked.

"Yeah. I'm scared, mommy." Luna's eyes were wide as she met Ida's gaze in the rearview mirror.

"It's going to be okay. Let's pray we aren't stuck." Ida put the car in reverse and gave it a little gas. The sound of the wheels spinning wasn't good. Her car rocked slightly, but it didn't move. They were at an angle that led her to believe she had done what she had hoped she wouldn't.

Landed in a ditch.

Ida put the car in park and rested her head back. She inhaled and glanced over at her phone. Luckily enough, it was on the charger and fully charged.

"Are we stuck?" Luna asked. "We have to

get home to Boots. I told him we wouldn't be gone long."

"It would appear so. Don't worry, babe. Boots will be fine." Ida took her hat off her head and tossed it onto the passenger seat. She reached for her phone and figured she'd call her father. He could at least come and get them. Her car could be towed out in the morning. She pulled up her father's number and placed the call.

Her phone was connected to her car's hands-free technology. The ringing filled the air. She waited and grew frustrated when it went to his voicemail.

"Okay," she murmured. She hung up and called her mother. Her call went immediately to voicemail. "What is going on?"

Ida sat back and looked at her phone. She contemplated calling her sister, but she was probably at work. She tried her father one last time, and again the call went to voicemail.

Ida glanced at her gas gauge and was thankful her car was full. She didn't know how long they could stay out here. She pulled up the internet and began scrolling for tow services.

"Are we going to have to wait long?" Luna asked.

"Hopefully not." Ida turned back and looked at her daughter. She offered her a smile, hoping it would comfort the worry she saw on Luna's face. "Put your gloves and hat on to keep warm. I'm going to see if we can get a tow truck to help us."

Ida just prayed they wouldn't take too long. She scanned the road and didn't see any lights from cars. Hopefully, a passerby would see her hazard lights. She'd hate to be the cause of a wreck.

She scanned her phone and pulled up a few local towing companies. Flashes of lights ahead of her caught her attention.

Was that someone coming down the road?

She sat up and took notice of the headlights. It looked like a pickup truck. Relief filled her. She flashed her lights in hopes they saw her. Whoever it was slowed down and stopped near her.

"I'll be right back, baby." Ida pulled her hat back on and her gloves. She yanked the zipper up to close her jacket completely.

"Mommy—"

"It's okay. I'm sure they will help us." Ida opened the door and stepped out into the storm.

2

Drew Bates tapped his hands to the beat of the rock song blaring on the radio. He had found the one channel not playing Christmas music. Not that he had anything against the holiday, it was just that holiday songs around the clock were starting to get old.

He was on his way home. He had locked up his clinic early with the threat of the storm. Looking at the white-out conditions surrounding them, he had made the right decision.

Drew, one of the local veterinarians, owned his clinic with his friend, Aiden Wallace. They had gone to veterinary school together, and once they had graduated, they bought and took over one of the local clinics from a retiring doctor.

Drew had grown up with a love of animals. From the time he could walk, he'd always owned a dog. His love of animals blossomed when he was in undergraduate school trying got figure out what he wanted to study.

His dog, Lucky, had passed away during his freshman year of school, and it was then he realized what he wanted to do with his life. He had always had a way with animals. He was the one person who, if someone had their dog or cat around, he would be talking to them.

Now he served to ensure animals led healthy lives, and here in Langdale, he was needed. There was another vet in town who specialized in big animals and usually took care of all the farms. Drew and Aiden specialized in the smaller animals. It worked out perfectly, and the two clinics didn't have to compete.

Currently, Drew was headed home. It was cold and snowing. All he wanted to do was get home, change his clothes, pour a drink, and watch a football game. His brother and family will be coming into town soon. Drew was sure his mother, Molly, would be putting them all to work for her annual holiday party.

Drew was a lucky son of a bitch. His family was extremely close, and the holidays were the time for them to all come together and celebrate family and love. His brother Harris lived in Chicago with his family. Growing up, he and Harris were as close as can be. They played on the same football team together, and while Drew went off to college, Harris had enrolled in the Marines. Drew was proud of his older brother. While he was deployed fighting for their freedom, Drew was in college. After completing his undergraduate program, he went on to veterinary school.

After graduation, he decided to move home. There was a great opportunity here for his practice, and his friend Aiden hadn't minded moving to Langdale.

"What the hell?" He squinted and saw the distinct yellow hazard lights of a car. It looked as if it was in a ditch. His conscious wouldn't allow him to drive past and not check on the person. Something in his gut had him braking and pulling over. He reached over and threw his hat and gloves on. It was freezing out, and he wasn't sure why anyone would be in this mess. The news had been talking about the storm all week.

Drew blew out a deep breath. He had chains in the back of his truck. He could hook them up and pull whoever this was out of the ditch. It would be his good deed for the day.

He threw his truck into park and exited it. The minute he stepped out of the vehicle, the wind slapped him on the face and took his breath away. He reached for the collar of his coat and brought it up to ward off the chill.

A small figure stood waiting by the driver's door of her car. He walked over to the car and took in the color and make of it. He recognized the vehicle.

No, it couldn't be.

He drew closer to the small individual huddle by the car.

"Ida?" he shouted.

"Drew, what are you doing out here?" Ida asked. Her frame shook while she stared up at him. Even in the darkness, with the only light coming from their cars, he could see their beauty.

He'd known this woman for years. She was the best friend of his sister-in-law. Ida and Gracie were a couple years older than him, graduating from high school with his brother. He remembered Ida from high school. She had been the knockout then. A cheerleader while he'd been a football player.

But she had never looked at him back then. What senior would be looking at a sophomore? He knew her to be shy, which attracted him to her. He always wanted to see her smile and to hear her laugh. She came around with her daughter, who was the exact image of her.

When Ida had purchased Boots for Luna, they had brought the pup to his clinic, and Boots became his patient.

"The question is why in the world are you out in this mess?" he asked. He moved closer to her so she could hear him. He bit back a growl at the sight of her shivering. He put an arm around her waist and drew her close to him. The wind began to pick up with a howl.

"We just came from seeing Santa," Ida shouted.

"They didn't cancel that?" he asked incredulously. Ida shook her head. He assumed Luna was in the car. Drew couldn't believe the town hadn't postponed their annual holiday event. Now he was glad he had stopped. Ida and Luna needed him. A weird feeling passed through his chest. He didn't know what it was, but he wanted to help Ida and Luna.

Luna was a sweet kid who cared for her pup, Boots. She was always a pleasure to have around. She and Grayson were always the center of attention at the Bates family home. His mother loved children and was getting on his case about finding someone to settle down with. Now that Harris had finally married Gracie, Molly Bates had focused her attention on Drew.

"You and Luna get in my truck. I'll get the chains, and we'll see if we can pull it out. If not, we'll leave it and have it towed out in the morning," he said. Ida nodded and moved away from him. He instantly missed the feeling of her against him. Even with their bulky coats on, and the frigid air between them, he still enjoyed having her near him. "I'll get Luna and put in her. I need you to put the car in neutral once I'm ready."

Ida hopped into the front seat while he opened the back door. Luna's head toward him. He saw her toothy grin and laughed.

"Hey, Luna."

"Uncle doctor!" Luna exclaimed. She thought because Harris was her 'uncle,' that meant he was too, and then with his additional title of animal doctor, she threw both together. "Are you here to save us?"

"I am. Let's get you into my truck. We will attempt to pull your mother's car out of this ditch." She nodded and unbuckled her seat belt. She slid across to him, allowing him to carry her. He held her close, her face buried into the base of his neck. He shut the door and trudged back over to his pickup. The snow falling picked up, swirling around in the air. He held on tight to not drop her. He slipped a few times in the snow but finally made it to his truck. He opened the door and helped her get into his quad cab's back seat. "Buckle up, buttercup."

"Okay." Luna scrambled into her seat and snapped her buckle in place.

He shut the door, went to the back of his truck, and grabbed his chains. He hooked them up to the back of Ida's car and then moved his truck behind her. He hopped back out into the elements and connected his truck to hers.

"Ida." He knocked on her window. She rolled the window down slightly. She looked so cute bundled up. Her smooth skin and warm brown eyes sent a wave of desire through him. He bit back a curse. This was not the time. He was surprised blood even went to his cock. The cold was biting through his jeans, and his thighs were already starting to numb. "Put the car in neutral. Once I start pulling you, I need you to guide it."

"Okay."

Drew jogged back to his truck and hopped in. He eyed Luna in the review mirror and sent her a wink. Her giggle filled the air. He had a soft spot in his heart for cute kids. One day he had hoped to have his own. He wouldn't dare say anything to his mother. She'd probably have every single woman in the town lined up at his door.

"Ready to pull your mother out?" he asked.

"Yes. We have to hurry and get home. Boots is probably worried about me," Luna said.

"All right then. Let's get your mother's car out so you two can get home." He threw his truck into reverse and gave it a little gas. Ida's car rocked, and his engine roared. He tightened his grip on his steering wheel while his truck tried to get her car out.

After several attempts, her car didn't budge.

He blew out a deep breath. The snow was coming down and piling up high. It would be best if he got the girls home where they could be safe. They could wait until the morning to have a tow truck get her out.

"Well, peanut. Your mother's car is really stuck. I'll be right back." He pushed open the door and stepped back into the elements. He walked over to Ida's car and knocked on her window again. She rolled it down slightly, disappointment lining her face.

"I'm not getting out tonight, am I?" she asked.

"No. Come on. I'll take you two home. Lock up." Ida jerked her head in a nod and rolled the window up. She cut the engine and opened the door. He helped her from the car. She grabbed a couple of bags from the back seat. He took them from her, kept one hand on her, and helped her to his truck. The snow was already up to their knees.

"Eek!" Ida screeched. She slipped and would have fallen flat on her face if he hadn't grabbed her by the back of her coat.

"Gotcha," he laughed. He yanked her back and pulled her close to him. She wrapped an arm around him and buried her face against his chest. He leaned down and rested his lips near her ear. "I won't let you fall."

"Please don't," she laughed. Drew guided her to the truck and helped her in. She took the two bags from him and put them in the back with Luna. Drew shut the door and jogged toward the driver's door. He jumped in and slammed the door shut. The wind's howling picked up.

"Everyone's buckled up?"

"Yes," Luna quipped from the backseat. He grinned at her and gave her a thumbs up.

"Good. Let's get you, ladies, home." He threw the truck into drive and slowly began the trek to their home.

They drove in silence with only the radio playing. Drew glanced over at Ida and found her watching him.

"Is something wrong?" he asked.

"No, I'm just hoping we weren't keeping you from anything since you are out in this crazy weather."

"I was just on my way home. We had closed the clinic due to the storm. That's why I was shocked you said the center was open."

"I got to see Santa," Luna said.

"Did you?" Drew met her gaze in the rearview mirror. He remembered what it was like to be a kid and sit on Santa's lap. He chuckled, thinking of how his brother had to sit in for Santa a couple years ago. "And did you tell him everything you wanted for Christmas?"

"Yup," Luna replied proudly.

"And you sure we are not taking you out of your way?" Ida asked.

"I'm positive. What am I supposed to do, leave you two here to wait for a tow? In these conditions, it would take all night for someone to get to you."

"Well, thank you. I really appreciate you stopping." Ida gave him a shy smile. She glanced down at her folded hands. He couldn't resist reaching out and taking her small hand in his. She glanced up at him with a shocked expression on her face. He squeezed her hand tight before letting go.

"It's my pleasure, Ida. I'd do anything for you. Just ask." Drew didn't know where that last part came from, but he meant it. He kept his attention on the road but felt Ida's eyes on him.

"Thanks, Drew. You're sweet."

The ride to her home was long and tortuous. Between the strong wind gusts, blinding snow, and the scent of Ida's perfume filling the air, Drew was going to go crazy. The longer he was in the truck with her, the more the desire to have her filled him.

Their conversations were never dull. Ida

shared stories about her job as a librarian, and he shared crazy stories of his animal clients. The sound of her laughter kept him hard the entire drive. This was the most time they had spent together that didn't include his brother and his wife or seeing Boots at his clinic.

Drew stole glances the entire drive. Even though he was fighting the snow drifts and wind, he couldn't help taking in Ida's smile. Her face lit up as she talked, and he was captivated by her.

They finally arrived at her home. The street was piled high with snow, with no plow truck in sight. Thankfully his vehicle had no problems driving down her road. He pulled into her driveway and put his truck in park.

"Finally," he breathed.

"I can't believe how long it took us to get here," Ida smiled. She turned around and looked at her daughter, who had fallen asleep. The ride, which should have taken about twenty minutes, took them over an hour.

"Don't worry. I'll get her and carry her in for you." Drew had noticed that Luna was practically the size of Ida. He didn't know how she would carry her in.

"Why don't you stay for dinner?" Ida asked. Her eyes grew wide while her teeth snuck out and nibbled her bottom lip. He had the sudden urge to want to lean in close and take a taste of those lips. "I put on chili in the crockpot. It should be done by now."

"I do love chili," he murmured.

"Then come in. It can be payment for saving us." She smiled at him, and his heart stuttered. He would be a fool to not stay. He glanced outside and took in the heavy snowfall. Big fat snowflakes fell from the sky. The windshield was already covered in the short time they had sat there.

"Lead the way."

3

Ida's hand shook as she slid her key into the lock. She pushed open the door and was immediately assaulted by the aroma of the meal she had left cooking. She loved using her crockpot, especially at this time of the year. She moved to the side to allow Drew to enter. He was carrying a sleeping Luna into the house.

Her heart pounded at the sight of her child in his arms. Had she been alone, she would have struggled to carry her sweet daughter, who slept like the dead. A bomb could go off, and Luna would sleep straight through the devastation. She dropped her bags and purse on the table behind her sofa.

"You can put her over here." Ida motioned to the couch. She was sure once Luna woke up, she would be starving. Her child was turning into an endless food pit. Ida shut the front door cutting off the cold air from blowing into her cozy place.

Boots, standing in his crate in the corner of the living room, greeted them with a few sharp barks.

"Hey, buddy," Drew laughed. He gently laid Luna down on the couch and began removing her shoes.

"I got her. Would you mind letting him out of his prison?" Ida jerked her head towards Boots, who was pacing in his cage.

"Sure thing." Drew walked over to boots while she sat down next to Luna. Boots' barking turned frantic. Ida tugged off Luna's boots and then began removing her coat. Luna didn't even open an eye. A snore slipped from the sleeping kid.

"I'm going to run him outside while you get her settled." Drew stood holding Boots. The black French bulldog was attempting to give Drew kisses.

"Really? Are you sure?" she asked in disbelief. She stood with Luna's jacket in her hand. Drew laughed at Boots' antics.

"It won't take long and will allow you a few minutes to do whatever you need to do." He eyed her while rubbing Boots on the head. Boots was practically purring in Drew's arms. The dog was resting against Drew's broad chest. Ida had never been jealous of a dog before. What she wouldn't give to be held by him and have other things stroked by his large hands.

"If you don't mind, his leash should be hanging inside the closet over there." Ida pointed to the closet near the front door. He jogged over and grabbed Boots' leash. The dog gave an approving bark before the two disappeared out the front door.

"Well, okay then," she giggled. She took her coat off, walked over to the same closet the leash was in and hung up her and Luna's jackets. She glanced one last time at her little sleeping beauty and went into the kitchen to check on their dinner. It wouldn't hurt for Luna to sleep a little longer while she got their plates together.

The aroma of her chili had her stomach

growling. She was thankful they were able to make it home safely.

Ida moved around her kitchen, gathered everything they would need for dinner, and walked into the dining room. It had been a long while since she had set her dining table for three, which included a member of the opposite sex she wasn't related to.

Butterflies fluttered in her stomach.

What if Drew didn't like her cooking?

She had eaten plenty of holiday dinner at his parents' home. Mrs. Bates was a woman touched by angels. There wasn't anything she couldn't cook, and now Ida was about to feed her son. Ida wasn't a bad cook, she enjoyed it, but she couldn't compare to Drew's mother.

She paused with the bowls in her hands and exhaled. This wasn't a date or anything. This was just Drew staying for dinner as payment for rescuing her and her daughter during a bad storm. She probably would have invited whoever would have brought them home. She moved to the counter where her crock pot sat and began filling their bowls. The front door opened, and stomping could be heard along with Boots' barking.

She ignored the flutter in her stomach. This was just Drew.

"I'll go ahead and call the tow trucks for you. I'm sure there will be a dozen calls from others who are stuck by morning. If I remember, Randy goes in the order the voicemails are left." Drew walked into the kitchen with his cell phone in his hand. Ida's hand paused with the ladle full of chili in the air. She stared at Drew. His dark hair was wet from the snow. It looked as if he had raked his fingers through it. He had removed his jacket and boots and for some reason seeing him standing in her kitchen in his socks had her lungs starving for air.

She blinked and inhaled.

"You didn't have to do that." Finally, her tongue was able to move. It had been stuck on the roof of her mouth the moment he stepped into the kitchen. She finished scooping Luna's chili into her bowl. Boots must have woken her up from the sounds of her daughter's giggle.

"I don't mind. I just sent Randy a text instead. Hopefully, he'll get to you first thing in the morning." Drew grinned. He slid his phone into his back pocket and stood by her. "Anything you need me to do?"

Holy mother of god.

Her ex-husband had never stepped foot in the kitchen to cook or help with anything. The only reason he ever stepped foot in the kitchen was to get a beer out of the fridge. The man always had blinders on when it came to the pile of dishes in the sink.

"Um, if you want to grab something to drink out of the fridge," She motioned to the fridge. She had some juices and sodas they could have with dinner. She didn't keep wine or alcohol in the house, which is a shame. With it being her and Luna, she just kept everything kid friendly. "I'll be in there in a moment."

"Sure thing. Me and Luna will wash our hands." Drew disappeared from the kitchen with the juice in his hand.

She closed her eyes briefly and had to calm her racing heart. This man was pushing all the rights buttons. By the time she entered the dining room, Luna and Drew were sitting at the table waiting for her. She quickly passed out their bowls and took her seat.

"This smells really good," Drew tossed her a wink before digging in. Ida smiled and lowered her eyes to her own food. They dug into the food, with Luna leading most of the conversation.

"Uncle Doctor, can you look at Boot's paw. He keeps licking it," Luna said.

"Sure. I can look at it before I leave," Drew said.

"There is nothing wrong with Boots' foot." Ida chuckled. According to Luna, there was always something wrong with the dog. Her daughter was very protective of her dog.

"But it is. He licked it twice this morning, then scratched his ear with it." Luna sat back in her chair, her lips beginning to pout.

"It's not a problem, Ida. I can look at Boots' paw." Drew glanced over at her. He wiped his mouth on his napkin and tossed it on the table. He lifted his glass and tipped it to her. "I tend to offer free exams for certain customers who have low income, and seeing how Luna is a full-time student, I'm sure she qualifies."

Ida snorted a laugh. She shook her head and saw that she wouldn't win this battle.

"I have some money I can pay you," Luna volunteered. Her eyes grew wide with hope.

"Don't worry, Luna bear. This visit will be free." Drew winked at Luna, who grinned.

"Okay, let's finish up dinner first." Ida had to put on her mom voice. Luna snapped to attention and went back to her food. She glanced around the table and, for a moment, wished that this was a typical night. She had been doing the single-parent thing for a moment, and it was getting old. She wished she could have someone to cuddle up with on nights like this after Luna went to bed. Her eyes met Drew's, and her heart skipped a beat.

She wished that person would be Drew.

"WILL UNCLE DREW BE STAYING THE night?" Luna's innocent question had Ida's mouth gaping open. She motioned for her daughter to get in bed. Drew had assessed his patient's foot and found it to be fine. His recommendation—a bath.

Luna promised she would give Boots a bath in the morning when she woke up.

"Why would you ask that?" Ida pulled the covers up over Luna. Her daughter's eyes were drooping low.

"Because he's here so late and all the snow. Can Uncle Doctor stay? Me and Boots like him."

Boots was snuggled in the bed with Luna. He gave a yip as if to agree with her daughter. Ida ensured Boots was under the blanket too.

"I'm sure Drew needs to get home. He did a lot for us today. I'm sure you will see him again," Ida murmured. She kissed Luna's forehead and reached over and rubbed Boots' head. "Now get some sleep. Both of you."

Ida stood and walked over to the door. She flipped the light switch, basking her daughter's room into darkness. Her small nightlight plugged into the wall was the only source of light. Luna shifted underneath her blanket, and only the top of her head was visible.

"I love you, momma," Luna's voice sounded so small. Ida smiled and blew her a kiss. She loved this little girl more than life itself. It broke her heart to think Luna was searching for a father figure to hold on to since hers was not involved in her daily life. Ida gave up trying to get that man to be involved with his daughter. All it led to were fights; she just didn't have it in her. She had promised herself that she would ensure that she was enough for her daughter.

"I love you too, Luna. See you in the morning." Ida left out of the room and shut the door behind her. She leaned back on it for a moment to gather herself. She pushed down the ache in her heart for her daughter. Then she glanced in the direction of the living room, and another part of her body began to ache. It had been a long while since she had been alone with a man as handsome and sexy as Drew. Her stomach was tied up in knots.

She blew out a deep breath and went back into the living room. She didn't see any signs of Drew. Maybe he already left. Disappointment filled her.

"He could have at least said goodbye, "she muttered. Maybe it was best he had left. There was no way he would be interested in her. He'd never shown any interest before and had always been friendly toward her and Luna. She moved over to the front door to ensure it was locked but found it slightly ajar.

Ida opened it and found Drew standing next to his truck. A gasp escaped her as she took in the snow that had fallen. Clumps of snow fell inside the house when she opened the door wider. The snow was midway up the side of his truck. The stairs to her porch were buried. Her yard had to have at least two to three feet of snow.

"I have a shovel if you want to try to dig yourself out," she said. Drew turned around at the sound of her voice. She was shocked to see the snow was mid-thigh on him. Drew backed a hefty laugh. How could so much fall so quickly? They had only been inside a few hours. The snow wasn't done. It still fell and quickly covered Drew as he stood in the yard. "It's in the garage."

"Even if I could dig myself out, I wouldn't be going anywhere. Look at the road," he replied. Drew slowly trudged through the depths of the snow. Ida scanned the area where the road should have been but couldn't see any trace of it, thanks to the snow.

It looked as if they were snowed in.

She swallowed hard at having Drew in her house all night.

"Looks like you're stuck with us tonight," she said. Her voice sounded husky to her ears. She cleared her throat and stepped back, holding the door open. She barely felt the cold. Her body was flushed, with so many naughty thoughts running through her head. Drew brushed past her, his gaze dropping down to her, with a smirk on his lips.

She shut the door and locked it. She turned, watching him remove his boots and jacket again. She moved aside so he could hang up his coat. Her body was completely aware of him. Her nipples hardened and pushed against her bra. It was a complete irritant, and she wanted to take it off.

Better yet, allow Drew to remove her from the offending contraption.

Inhaling, she folded her arms in front of her. Those types of thoughts were going to get her into trouble. Since she and Luna moved into this home, there hadn't been a man who had spent the night.

It would look like Luna would get her wish.

"I hope you don't mind," Drew said. His eyes darkened as they narrowed in on her. She offered a smile and shrugged.

"Of course. It's been a long time since I had an adult sleepover." Her eyes widened at her joke. Her face warmed from embarrassment. She slid past him and walked back into the living room. His deep chuckle followed behind her.

"A sleepover sounds fun. Haven't done that since I was a kid. Will there be games, hot cocoa, and stories by the fire?" Drew teased.

Ida's glanced at her gas fireplace on the wall and motioned to it.

"You start the fire, and I'll go make us some hot cocoa?" She walked backward with him advancing on her. She swallowed hard, seeing a devious glint in his eyes.

Was that desire for her?

Was he having the same thoughts she was?

Drew raked his fingers through his hair, knocking some trapped snowflakes from his thick strands. She wished it was her fingers sliding through his damp hair, pushing it away from his face. Her breath caught in her throat at the fantasy that was coming to play.

"Sounds good to me." He brushed past her, not touching her. The scent of him assaulted her, and Ida knew she was in trouble. She spun around and headed into the kitchen.

"Get yourself together," she muttered. She bustled around the kitchen, making their drinks. She reached for two matching mugs and set them on the counter while she warmed up their milk.

She rested her hands on the counter and closed her eyes.

Breathe, girl.

This was a friendly thing to do by allowing him to spend the night. Come morning, the snow trucks will have cleared the streets enough for him to leave. A tightening sensation spread across her chest.

She didn't want him to go. From the short time he'd spent with her and Luna, Ida had to agree.

She wanted him here come morning.

But not to leave.

That look in his eye had been for her. She knew beyond a doubt that he had some feelings for her. He wanted her, just as she wanted him.

Ida glanced down at herself and groaned. Nothing she had on would be considered sexy. She had been dressed as a practical mom taking her daughter to see Santa.

Who knew the object of her desires would fall in her lap?

Ida wasn't going to pass up a chance to make her feelings known. She'd find a way to tell Drew.

What was the worse that could happen?

He'd say he wasn't interested and you had read everything wrong?

Ida shook her head and refused to believe her conscious. She finished making their drinks and topped them with a hefty amount of whip cream.

"Here we go," she murmured. She carried the two mugs into the living room. Drew had the fire going. She noticed that he'd even turned off the lamp, leaving them in the dark with only the fire providing a soft light to the room. He'd opened the bay window allowing them to view the perfect winter wonderland outside.

Her heart leaped in her chest.

It was the perfect scenario to address what was weighing heavy on her chest.

She handed Drew his and then took the seat next to him.

"Oh, my. This looks good," Drew chuckled and took a sip.

Ida held her cup with both hands to give them something to do. She didn't want to risk one of them being free and do something like rest on his thigh or reach up to brush that lock of hair from his forehead.

"I hope it's not too sweet," she said. Ida would have to admit she had a sweet tooth and could overdo it sometimes.

"No, it's perfect." He moved the cup from his face and licked his lips. She giggled, staring at the dollop of whip cream resting on the tip of his nose. He grinned at her. "What's so funny?"

"You have a little something...." She moved closer to him on the couch before she could even think of it. She reached up and wiped his nose with her finger. She held it up to show the cream before licking her finger clean. Drew's eyes darkened as he stared at her mouth. "There. Got it."

4

Drew was transfixed on Ida's plump lips. Staying the night at her house was going to be very interesting. This woman had been on his mind for a while now, and the attraction between them was sizzling. The air stifling with sexual tension and lust. Now she was pressed close to him. He could feel the warmth of her body. Her big brown eyes grew wider when he gently took her mug and set it on the coffee table with his.

He reached for her and brought her astride his lap. She didn't resist. A sigh escaped her, confirming what he'd known.

She wanted him just as he wanted her.

He shouldn't be touching her. This was

his sister-in-law's best friend. Someone who had been innocently flirting with him since the day they met.

Now he had her in his arms.

Everything felt right about this moment.

Why had he waited so long to let his intentions and thoughts be known?

Now, Ida would know how he truly felt about her.

He cupped her face and brought it down to his, taking her mouth in a soft, gentle kiss. Drew captured her moan as she surrendered to his kiss. His tongue pushed into her mouth and got his first taste of her. She was sugary and sweet, just like hot cocoa. He thought of nothing but her warmth and knew that the rest of her would be just as addicting.

Ida's arms wrapped around his neck. Her body melted against his, her knees resting along his side on the couch. The kiss deepened, and his hands slid along her thighs and settled on her ample ass. He pulled her to him, closing the gap between them. He needed to feel all of her.

Drew wanted Ida naked so he could explore every inch of her and taste all she was. He tore his mouth from hers. He smirked at the little whimper of protest that escaped her lips. He trailed kisses along her jawline and down the soft curve of her neck. Her full breasts were crushed against his chest. He hand skated underneath her sweater and found the clasp of her bra. He flicked it, undoing it in mere seconds.

They were about to cross a line. It would take him another few seconds to take off this offending top and contraption and bare her to him.

"Tell me you want me," he rasped. Drew pulled back slightly to look at her. Ida's eyes were closed, her breaths coming in pants. Those beautiful brown orbs fluttered opened and locked on his. She pressed her core against his waist, slightly rocking her bottom along his erection. His cock was engorged and demanding release from its captivity.

A growl ripped from him as she teased him.

Her fingers threaded their way into his thick hair. She held tight, a smile appearing on her kiss-swollen lips.

"Stay the night with me." It wasn't a question or a request. It was a soft demand that he was only too willing to oblige. She sprinkled kisses along my face in the direction of my cheek. She leaned over and whispered in my ear, "Let's go into my room."

She didn't need to repeat herself.

Drew easily lifted her as he stood from the couch. The sound of Ida's giggle went straight to his already stiff cock. It swelled even more as she settled against him with her legs wrapping around his waist.

"Which one is yours?" he rasped. He stalked toward the hallway with his hands full of Ida's ass. He couldn't wait to strip her of her clothing and lie her down on the bed where he could see all of her.

"That one," she whispered. Drew followed the direction in which she pointed. He assumed one of the other doors led to Luna's room. He didn't have much experience rearing children, but it was apparent with Luna's room so close to Ida's that they would need to keep it down.

Just the thought of having quiet sex and the threat of not being caught had him rushing into her room. Her domain smelled of her sweet perfume. The room was on the smaller side but held a bed that took up most of the room. A nightstand was on one side of the bed with a lamp left on. Her windows were adorned with sheer curtains that allowed some of the moonlight to shine in. The room was feminine and all Ida.

He nudged the door closed with his foot, not willing to put Ida down until they were standing next to the bed. Ida slowly slid down the length of him. Drew bit back a curse at the feeling of her soft, supple body.

"Are you sure?" he hooked his fingers at the edge of her sweater. He had to make sure. If she changed her mind, he would leave immediately.

Ida smirked and brushed his hands away. She lifted her sweater and tossed her bra onto the floor next to them. Drew was rendered frozen for a moment. His gaze swept her soft, curvy frame from her wide brown eyes to her sound mounds. Her areolas and nipples were a darker shade of brown. Her nipples were perky and erect, begging for his attention. Her belly held a slight pudge, but he could care less. The woman had birthed a child.

His throat constricted at the thought. He moved forward, resting his hand on her stomach. The image of her swollen with his child flashed before him. His breath was ripped from his chest at the thought. He brought his gaze back to hers and tipped her chin upwards. He leaned down and covered her mouth with his.

Her mouth immediately opened to his. The kiss grew frantic the second his tongue connected with hers. Ida moaned, leaning into him. He cupped her face holding her in place. Drew lifted his head, his hands sliding down to her jeans. Hers joined his, and together they stripped each other from their clothing. He stood before Ida with no shame in how he presented.

"Jesus!" she swore under her breath, her gaze locked on his cock. He smirked at the hungry look in her eyes. He lifted her up, laid her across the bed, and braced himself over her.

"Don't worry. I won't hurt you," he murmured jokingly. He positioned himself in between her thighs. He was larger than average and promised to take it slow and steady with her. He wanted to take his time and appreciate the fight that she was giving him. She wrapped her arms around his neck, her mouth curving into her sexy grin.

"Oh, I'm not complaining. I want everything you can give me."

Drew growled and swooped down, taking her lips in a harsh, brutal kiss. He didn't know where the shy and coy Ida went, but he wouldn't complain. He liked when a woman voiced what she wanted.

His body was flooded with heat. Her fingers dove into his hair, gripping it tight. Her soft moans drove him crazy. His cock was swollen and ready to sink into her warm channel. He tore his mouth from hers, his attention locked on her full breasts. He took one into his hand while licking the other with his tongue. Her taut pebbled nipple was sweet as he knew it would be. He teased, suckling the one while his hand grasped and kneaded the other. He soon switched, taking his time getting familiar with them both.

"Drew," her soft whisper sent a white-hot need through him. He wanted to hear her scream his name, but tonight would not be the night since her daughter was asleep in the next room. Her foot slid along his calf while her hand moved along the back of his neck.

Drew ignored her, continuing his journey south. He wanted her spread out before him so he could breathe in her scent. Taste her. Give her an immense amount of pleasure. He arrived at her core and pushed her thighs apart, presenting her to him. He sucked in a quick breath, taking in her plump lower lips, slick entrance, and protruding nub. Her clit was swollen and demanding his attention. Drew wasted no time in parting her labia and taking his first taste of her.

His tongue slid along her slit. Her slickness gathered on his tongue. The taste of her exploding in his mouth. Her body arched off the bed, but he pushed her down with one hand.

"Drew," she called out his name again.

"Tell me what you want, Ida," he drawled. He snuck his tongue out and flicked her clit with it. The move elicited another moan from her. He captured the bud and began to suckle it. She cried out, and the sound drove him to a frenzy. He yanked her by her hips and pulled her further to him, pressing his hands on her thighs to keep her open.

He feasted on Ida. There was no other way to describe it. Her taste was an aphrodisiac to him. He couldn't get enough. Her fingers tighten in his hair painfully. He didn't care if he'd be bald by the morning. Her body shook underneath him. Drew's cock was painfully hard pressing against the mattress. He rocked his hips slightly as a groan slipped from him. He needed to be balls deep inside of her but refused until she reached her climax.

Ida's hips bucked, allowing her to thrust her pussy further into his mouth. He grinned at the fact that his little quiet Ida was turning into a ferocious sex kitten. Her gasps and groans were sexy. He reached up and took one of her breasts in his hands while he continued to suck on her clit. He tugged and pulled on her nipple, causing her to cry out.

Soon, her body was trembling uncontrollably. Drew pushed a finger inside of her. Ida's slickness coated his finger. He thrust it in slowly, fucking her how he wished he could do with his cock.

Soon.

Drew tightened his hand on her breasts while he applied a sweet pressure to her clit, tugging it simultaneously. Ida threw her head back, a silent scream erupting from her. Her warm release slipped from her, coating his hand and his mouth. Pride filled Drew's chest.

He had given her one hell of a climax. He didn't have to hear her scream. He felt it in the way her body arched toward the ceiling, to the way it trembled to the warm cream slipping from her center. Ida flopped back onto the bed, panting. Drew grinned and took another swipe at her pussy with his tongue before pushing up from the bed. He crawled over her and nudged her opening with his cock.

Ida's eyes fluttered open and met his. A sexy smirk appeared on her lips.

"Give it to me," she whispered.

"What happened to shy Ida?" he asked.

She shrugged her shoulders and chuckled.

"She's here. You just haven't gotten to

know this side of me," she breathed. He pushed forward, sinking inside of her. Drew bit back a groan. Ida's pussy was slick, warm, and tight. He grunted, pausing for a moment. Ida whispered sweet nothings, encouraging him to move.

He opened his eyes, maintaining her gaze until he was fully seated inside her. He gripped the blankets tightly and tried to will his body to calm down. He wanted to pound away into her until he lost himself completely.

But if he did that, he wouldn't last long at all.

A shudder rippled through him. With careful control, he pulled out until only the tip of his cock remained inside her before thrusting home.

"Ida," her name was ripped from him. Her thighs squeezed his waist. She brought them up higher, allowing him to sink further inside her. Drew grunted, increasing the rhythm of his hips. Ida's hands rested on his ass, pulling him to her.

"You can't break me," she whispered.

"Fuck. You can't say shit like that," Drew rasped. Her deep-throated chuckle was her only response. He was drowning in her dark brown pools. He lifted her leg higher, changing their position. She cried out in pleasure, her eyes snapped shut while her head rested back against the bed. Drew rocked harder, pushing even deeper inside of her. The new angle gave him more authority over their pleasure. Her wetness coated him, allowing him to thrust with ease.

An animalistic nature overcame him. He wanted to claim this woman. Make her his.

He gripped her hair with his other hand, tilting her head away to expose her neck. He bent down, licking and nipping her soft, satiny skin. His mouth latched onto her neck, suckling it hard. He wanted to leave his mark on her. Something barbaric inside of him wanted to see her skin marred by him. Her mounds were crushed between them. Her short, small gasps of pleasure sent him spiraling even more toward the edge of his orgasm.

He had to hold out. He refused to reach his release before her.

He didn't have long to wait.

Ida's muscles grew tense. He released her neck just as her inner walls clamped down on his. Her mouth dropped open in a soundless scream. Her nails bit into his flesh, but he ignored the pain.

The pleasure mounted as her pussy began to milk him.

Drew reached his release.

A groan started deep in his chest and was making its way out. Drew no longer controlled his hips as they pounded against Ida's. His balls drew up close as a warm rush of pleasure rippled through his body. His hand tightened on her hair, unable to let it go. His body went taut as he began to fill her with his seed.

A strangled cry escaped him.

Ida's hand slapped onto his mouth to silence him.

Fuck.

He'd forgotten Luna was in the room next door, but his body was not cooperating. His hips continued to thrust, sending his release deep inside of her. Ida's pussy welcomed everything he had to give, contracting tight around him.

Finally, he stopped moving and had to keep himself from crashing onto Ida.

"I'm sorry," he muttered against her

hand. Her low laughter filled his ears. He opened his eyes, barely able to control his breathing. She stared at him with a lopsided grin on her lips.

"Oh, that's quite all right. I just don't want to have the birds, and the bees talk with my child in the morning." His dick twitched inside of her. It was still semi-hard. Her smile slowly faded.

"Are you still—

He captured her lips in a slow, deep kiss. Her arms wrapped around him and held him to her. She was a temptation that he wasn't ready to be done with. He pulled back from her, dropping small kisses on her lips and chin.

"There's no rush," he murmured. He withdrew from her warm heat and rolled to his side, taking her with him. She slid into the crook of his arm, resting her head back so they could see each other. Drew arranged the covers over them and ensured her body was flushed against his. Her warm, curvy body fit perfectly against his. He could quickly get used to this. "Our slumber party is just getting started. We have all night."

5

"Mommy."

Ida frowned. She was amidst a steamy dream where Drew was behind her. She bit her lip and sighed. Why would Luna be in this dream?

"Mommy, wake up."

Ida's breath froze in her chest. She cracked open one eye and found her daughter kneeling beside her bed. Her playful big brown eyes were staring at her waiting for her to wake up.

"Hey, baby. I'm up." Ida held the blanket to her naked frame as she sat up slightly. She held back a wince from the discomfort between her legs. It was a welcome pain when she thought of her night with Drew. He was larger than she had expected, but she was only too happy to jump up to the challenge of accepting him.

Speaking of Drew.

She glanced over at the side of the bed he'd slept on. Not that there was much sleeping. She breathed a sigh of relief. Eventually, there would need to be a discussion of the birds and bees with Luna, but this morning wouldn't have been the time.

"Uncle Doctor is cooking breakfast and told me to wake you up so we can eat," Luna giggled.

"He did what?" Ida gasped. The man had rocked her world last night and was thoughtful enough to not be in her bed when her daughter woke up and cooked breakfast.

She was practically in love.

"He made pancakes and stuff. Come on, mommy. I'm hungry." Luna tugged at her hand, trying to get her out of bed.

"Okay. I'm coming. Let me throw some clothes on. I'll be right there," Ida promised.

"Okie dokie." Luna skipped out of the room and shut the door behind her. Ida swung her legs to the side of the bed and winced once she stood. Muscles she didn't remember having screamed at the torture of her walking to her closet. She wouldn't have time for a quick shower. She threw on a pair of leggings and a t-shirt. She rushed to the bathroom and almost hollered at her reflection. She looked like a woman who had been well fucked. Her hair stood up everywhere, her eyes looked glazed over, and her erect nipples were overly sensitive. Her cotton shirt was wreaking havoc on them. A shiver rippled down her spine. Maybe she should put a bra on.

She groaned at the thought. What sane woman wore a bra in her own house? She quickly scrapped that idea. Drew had licked, sucked, and touched every inch of her body. Ida's gaze fell to her neck where Drew had marked her. She hadn't had a hickie since she was much younger. She reached up and gently caressed the darkened area. Her core clenched from the memory that appeared.

There was nothing she needed to hide from him. She quickly made herself presentable before leaving out of the bathroom.

Ida's stomach growled. She made her way into the kitchen. Her feet paused at the entrance as she took in Drew standing in front of her stove. Music played from his phone that sat on the counter. His head bopped to the beat while he flipped a couple of pancakes over. Her heart thumped wildly at the sight. He was dressed in jeans, a t-shirt, and bare feet.

Ida bit her lip at how sexy he looked cooking. There was something about a man who knew his way around a kitchen.

"Good morning." Ida cleared her throat. Drew glanced over his shoulder, a smile spreading on his lips. He took the pancakes off, placed them on the plate with the other, and shut off the stove. He turned around and leaned back against the counter.

"Nah, you can do better than that." He waved his fingers for her to come to him. Her feet had a mind of their own. She found herself moving across the kitchen and into his arms. Drew's large hands cupped her cheeks while he lowered his head. Their lips met in a slow, sweet kiss that had her melting against him. "Now that's better."

Ida blinked her eyes, trying to get them to focus. She wrapped her arms around his waist and smiled.

"Good morning," she said again. "Thanks for —

"You don't have to say anything. I figured it wouldn't be best for Luna to find us in the bed naked." He grinned. He dropped another kiss on her lips. "I figured you could tell her about us another way."

"There's an us?" she whispered.

"If you have to question my intentions after last night, I must not have done it right." He wrapped her up in his arms and held her to him. His smile slowly faded as he studied her. "Do you want there to be an us?"

She jerked her head into a nod.

"Then I'll make sure to show you again tonight." He planted another kiss on her lips. It was then Ida picked up the sound of giggling behind them. She turned and found Luna peeking her head into the doorway. A side smile was on her face as she watched the two of them. "Come get in on this hug, pipsqueak."

Luna raced across the room with Boots in tow. Drew and Ida opened their arms to her and included her. Boots barked, circling them, demanding to be let into the circle.

"Are you hungry, baby?" Ida asked. She blinked back her tears at the emotions running through her. Luna didn't really know her father well and hadn't spent much time with him as of late. Luna's tiny arms were wrapped tight around them.

"I'm starving. Can you two kiss later? My belly is grumbling," Luna said. She released them and picked Boots up, who wiggled and barked.

"We can eat," Drew laughed.

Ida and Luna set the table, and soon they were eating, enjoying the delicious breakfast that Drew had cooked. Laughter filled the air, giving Ida a sense of a family. This was the type of life she wanted for her daughter. Drew and Luna were cracking jokes and talking about the animals he takes care of. He was filled with stories that kept a smile on her and Luna's faces.

"Can I, mommy?" Luna asked, turning her attention to Ida.

Ida blinked, having missed the conversation and question.

"What's that?" she asked.

"Uncle Doctor invited me to come and watch at the animal clinic," Luna said.

"Well, first, I think you can call him Drew," Ida said. She cleared her throat and reached for her coffee mug. She took a sip before setting it down. "And I think that sounds fun as long as you're supervised."

Drew's clinic saw more than dogs and cats. There had been plenty of times they had been waiting for Boots' appointment and saw lizards and snakes. She shivered at the memory of a giant boa constrictor in the waiting room.

"Of course. She won't leave my side," Drew winked at Luna.

"Okay, then, sure." Ida breathed a sigh of relief. She had a vivid imagination and would hate to explain to her parents that her daughter was taken out by a snake or something worse at an animal clinic.

"Speaking of my clinic. I need to see if I can get out. We were supposed to be open today." Drew pushed back from the table and stood. He began clearing the table by piling their plates up on his.

"Don't worry about the dishes. I can get to them." Ida stood and followed him into the kitchen with her mug and silverware.

"No need. I clean as I cook. These I'm sure we can just toss in the dishwasher."

Could this man be even more perfect?

"I'll load it—

"Mom, Boots has to pee. Can we just let him out in the yard?" Luna called out from the door. Boots barked and ran back and forth through the doorway.

"Go. I can do this." Drew shooed her out of her kitchen. She was not used to this at all.

She laughed and spun around and went with Luna. They bundled up in their boots, winter coats, hats, gloves, and scarves. It was bitter cold outside, and a ton of snow. She opened the door and didn't see how Boots, as small as he was, would manage.

"Hold on, baby. Let me get a shovel and make a path for Boots." She opened the garage, grabbed one of the shovels, and began a path from the front steps down to her driveway. She was out of breath by the time she was done. The snow wasn't the light, fluffy kind. It was heavy and was going to be hell to move. Luna waited at the door with Boots on his leash. "Come on. Bring him down."

Luna and Boots made their way down the stairs so he could handle his business. Ida glanced around her yard and shook her head. There was so much snow, and it engulfed Drew's truck. She couldn't even see the wheels.

"Mom," Luna came to stand next to her. Boots stood near the edge of a pile of snow and lifted his leg, marking his territory.

"Yes, baby?" she asked. She reached for Luna and brought her close. She kissed the top of her daughter's head.

"Is Uncle...Drew, your boyfriend now?" Luna asked. Ida paused, thinking of the answer. Drew had already put his claim on her. A warmth spread through her at the thought. She smiled softly, studying Luna's curious face.

"What would you think of it?" she asked instead. She wanted to gauge her daughter's reaction first. Luna was number one in her life. She would never want to do anything that would harm her or hurt her feelings.

"He's cool, and he makes you laugh a lot. I like him." Luna gave an approving nod. Ida wasn't sure when her daughter became so observant. "Boots!"

The French bulldog jerked away from Luna. His leash trailed behind him as he took off down the path Ida had carved out of the snow then he promptly disappeared into the snow.

"Boots!" Ida yelled out. She and Luna took off behind him. Her daughter frantically called out his name. His muffled bark replied to her. Somehow, he had made it to the middle of their yard. "Dammit."

Ida took off as fast as she could, fighting against the high snow that came up to her thighs.

"What's wrong?" Drew asked from behind her.

"Boots is lost in the snow," Luna cried out. "He's going to get frozen."

"I'm almost to him. I see him," Ida grunted. She lifted her legs one at a time and prayed she didn't fall over. The little black dog yipped again, and she was almost to him. Divots appeared in the snow, revealing where he was. She finally made it to him. Ida scooped up the trembling pup and held him up in the air. "Got him!"

She spun around and tried to return to where Luna and Drew stood. Her foot snagged on something, and down she went. She cursed and tried to push herself up but kept slipping down. Boots barked frantically while wiggling to get away from her.

"Hold still, dammit." Ida was fighting a losing battle with the dog. He was determined to get free of her hold. Snow surrounded her. She shook her head to remove the snow that had flown into her face. It was getting everywhere. The cold stuff somehow slid down into her coat, and her leggings weren't meant to be dipped in snow. Wetness began to seep through the thin material. She'd laugh at the situation if she wasn't still half-buried.

"Here, let me help you." Large hands gripped her coat and lifted her from the snow. Drew grinned as he helped her stand. He brushed snow off her face and coat before falling into a fit of laughter.

"Fine. Laugh at me if you want." She cradled Boots to her chest and began walking toward the porch with Drew's help. Her lips curled up into a smile. They made it to the edge, where she handed Boots off to Luna. "Take your dog inside and help get him warm."

"Is he going to be okay?" Luna asked. Her brows dipped down into a frown.

"I'll look him over when I get inside. Get him a warm blanket and rub him down," Drew said.

"Okay." Luna spun around and went into the house.

"She was only worried about the dog?" Ida gasped. She saw where her daughter's loyalty was. Her small french bulldog.

"She's just a kid thinking she was about to lose her best friend." Drew brought her closer to him. He plopped one hell of a kiss on her that had her toes curling in her boots. "Go inside and get warm. I'll handle the driveway before we leave."

"Leave?" Ida blinked her eyes, trying to stay focused. The man's kisses left her a puddle of a mess.

"Randy left me a message that he towed your car to his shop since we didn't answer this morning." He grinned and took her hand in his. He guided her over to the stairs.

"You sure you don't want me to help you with the driveway?" she asked. There was a lot of snow, and it would go quicker if they worked together.

"Woman, you are drenched, and I'm sure cold. No need for hyperthermia to set in. Go inside." He pressed another kiss to her lips. His eyes darkened in a way that had her shivering, and it wasn't because of the cold. "I got this."

She nodded and went inside.

Yes, she could get used to this.

Hell, she was already halfway in love with the man.

❧ 6 ❧

"Hey, ma." Drew walked into his parents' kitchen. He knew where he would find her in the kitchen prepping for their annual Christmas Eve party. Ever since the first night he had spent with Ida, they had been together non-stop. Their relationship was a whirlwind, but he wouldn't have it any other way. She constantly filled his mind, and he couldn't get enough of her.

Molly Bates was going to be over the moon to find out her other son was now in a relationship.

Not just a casual one at that. Drew had come to have strong feelings for Ida and

Luna. His hand shook as he raked his fingers through his hair.

Drew knew he was in love with both of them. Luna was a fresh breath of air. When he thought of having a daughter, that little girl would be her. She was silly, crazy, intelligent, and beautiful, just like her mother. She brought a smile to his lips, remembering the sound of her laughter.

"Hey, Drew." Molly was mixing something in a bowl. Her preparations for tomorrow's party were already underway. She turned and hugged him with one arm. "Don't think you are showing up a day early to steal something to eat."

He laughed as she wagged a finger at him. He moved over to her and engulfed her in a tight hug. She turned her face so he could plant a kiss on her cheek.

"If I got to wait, then so do you." Harris ambled into the room. Drew's older brother grinned and came over to him. Then did their brotherly hug and slapping on the back.

"When did you get into town?" Drew asked.

"About an hour ago. We were supposed to come yesterday, but Grayson had an upset stomach yesterday." Harris beamed at the mention of his son. Drew could admit he was envious of his older brother. Harris had fallen in love with his best friend, Gracie. Anyone with eyes could see the two were meant to be together. It just took them growing up and living life to come to the conclusion themselves. Drew loved his sister-in-law like a sister. His nephew was the apple of his eye. Grayson Bates was as handsome as all the Bates men and already had everyone in the family wrapped around his little finger.

"Is everything okay?" Drew asked.

"Oh, yeah. Gracie thinks it was one of those twenty-four-hour bugs. He's back to driving us crazy," Harris laughed.

"Harris, honey. Can you grab a few sticks of butter and put them on the counter so they can start softening. I don't think I have enough," Molly directed. Harris strolled to the fridge while Molly turned her attention back to Drew. Her eyes twinkled as she studied him. Their mother loved to entertain. Any excuse to get family together for the holidays. "Did you want to tell me something?"

"Yeah, actually, I do." Drew scratched the back of his neck and cleared his throat. He grinned and figured he'd just tease her a little. "I hope you don't mind if I bring someone to the party tomorrow."

"What?" His mother's eyes grew wide. "Who? You've never brought anyone. Is this a friend or someone you work with? Is it Aiden? I've been telling you for years to bring that boy—"

"Mom." Drew laughed and rested his hands on her shoulders. Her excitement had him smiling.

"You've done it now. Put her out of her misery and tell her who it is," Harris chuckled. He set the butter down on the counter. "Trust me."

"Well, Aiden did accept the invite and will be coming, but I'm bringing someone else. Someone special to me," Drew admitted.

"Who is that?" Harris frowned.

"Who is who?" Gracie breezed into the room empty-handed. She tucked her hair behind her ear and came over to join them.

"Where's my nephew?" Drew asked, deflecting the questions.

"With his pop pop," Gracie laughed. "Chester has him in front of the television, teaching him all about his beloved football."

Chuckles went around the room. No one got in between Chester Bates and his football. The retired sheriff's deputy loved his favorite recliner and television.

"Drew, you never answered me. Who are you bringing to the party?" Molly asked, whacking him on the arm with the back of her hand.

Not wanting to spill the beans now, Drew grinned, walked over to the fridge, and took out a few long-neck beers. One for him and one for his father.

"My girlfriend." He quickly slipped from the kitchen, ignoring his mother's squeal and the calling of his name. He'd let her stew until tomorrow. He entered the family room where his father and nephew were exactly where Gracie said they would be. "What's up, pops?"

Drew took a seat on the small sofa next to his father. He remembered many days of sitting in the same spot Grayson was in.

Chester Bates was one hell of a father. He spent all the time he could with Harris and Drew when he was not working long shifts. Their father was a dedicated man who had given forty years of his life to protecting their town.

Now that he was retired, he got to enjoy life and drive his wife crazy.

Drew had learned everything he knew about being a man from his father. He had always looked up to the old man.

"Oh, nothing. Watching the game." He took the beer Drew handed him. He glanced back at Drew. "How am I supposed to drink this?"

"I got you, dad. A certain someone ran out of the kitchen after dropping an announcement on mom," Harris chuckled. He came into the room holding up the opener.

"She'll be okay," Drew replied sheepishly. Harris popped open their father's beer before sitting next to Drew. After opening his own, he passed the device to Drew.

"She will be talking nonstop until you tell her who it is." Harris leaned back on the couch. The game captivated all three men, even young Grayson. Their shouts filled the room when their team scored. They cheered and laughed. Even Grayson clapped his hands.

Once they settled down, Chester turned to Drew.

"What announcement?" Chester asked.

"He told mom he was bringing someone to the party tomorrow," Harris snorted.

"A woman?" Chester asked.

"I'm bringing my girlfriend over for everyone to meet," Drew admitted.

"A mysterious girlfriend that he hadn't even told me about." Harris nudged him with his elbow.

"It just happened," Drew admitted. He glanced down at the cold beer in his hand and smiled. He couldn't wait to share with his family that he and Ida was an item. They already loved her. She usually came to the party as a guest of Gracie, but this year, she would be with him. "Don't worry. You're going to love her."

"**I**'m so nervous," Ida whispered. This wasn't the first time she'd attended a holiday party at the Bates' home, but it would be the first time attending as Drew's girlfriend. She bit her lip and stared at the scenery as it passed by.

Drew had picked her and Luna up in his truck, not trusting the weather or her small sedan. The town had been bombarded with a few feet of snow since the initial snowstorm.

"There's nothing to worry about." Drew reached over and took her hand in his, entwining their fingers together. They were on their way to his family's home, and the butterflies were taking over her stomach. He turned onto the street where his parents lived.

"What do you mean? We're telling your family that we are together. What if they have only liked me because of Gracie?" She closed her eyes and didn't know how she would take it if they didn't like the thought of her with their son.

"Of course, they like you," Drew laughed. He pressed a kiss to the back of her hand. She softened and relaxed. He just had that way about him. The past week had been magical. They had spent all their time together when they weren't working. "We are here."

He parked his truck on the road in front of the house. There were multiple cars lined up along the street. Ida stared at the house and blew out a deep breath.

Gracie had invited her and Luna. She had promised she would be there. Ida hadn't told her friend she was coming as Drew's date. She remembered when she'd found out about Gracie and Harris. She had been a little hurt, but ultimately, she was relieved that the two finally realized they were in love.

Drew exited the vehicle and helped Luna first before coming to help her. Ida felt terrible for not bringing anything to the party. She was sure Mrs. Bates had cooked up enough food to feed an army, and Gracie was probably in the thick of things helping. Her friend had a real passion for baking.

"And don't worry. I told them I was bringing my girlfriend," Drew winked at her.

"You did what?" she gasped. Drew snagged Luna's hand and began walking toward the house. He and Luna laughed and giggled at something he said that Ida couldn't catch.

This man was going to drive her crazy.

She scurried along behind them to the house. Drew opened the door so Luna could go in first. Ida already knew her daughter would be looking for baby Grayson. They entered the house and stopped at the closet near the foyer. Drew helped them out of their coats and boots before taking Ida's hand.

"Can I go find Grayson?" Luna asked.

"Of course, baby. Make sure to speak to everyone." Ida pressed a kiss to her daughter's forehead.

Drew rested a hand on her hip and brought her to him. His bright blue eyes studied her while his lips curved up into a smile.

"Ready?" he murmured.

"Nope, but let's get this over with."

"That's my girl." He dropped a kiss on her lips.

"Drew's here," Harris's deep voice called out behind her. Ida jumped but Drew held her to him. She turned and found Harris grinning at the two of them. "Well. I'll be damn."

"What's up, big brother," Drew greeted his brother calmly.

"Now I see why there were secrets." Harris barked a laugh. "Mom and Gracie are going to love this."

"Love what?" Gracie ambled over to her husband. She stopped abruptly. Her gaze flicked between Drew and Ida. Recognition appeared in her eyes. "Seriously? You two?"

Ida braced herself, unsure of how her friend would take this. They hadn't spoken this week except for a few text messages, but Ida hadn't shared with her friend that she was involved with Drew.

"Yeah." Ida rested her hand along Drew's, which had moved to her stomach. She looked up at him, a smile on her lips. She was the happiest she had ever been and hoped her friend was okay with this. Drew pressed a soft kiss to her lips to solidify the answer.

"I'm so happy for you!" Gracie squealed. She rushed over to them, pushing Drew out of the way so she could wrap her arms around Ida. They laughed and danced together. Gracie knew all about her failed marriage and her relationship with her ex-husband.

"Thank you," Ida said.

"Now go find Molly before that woman wears a hole in the floor with her pacing." Gracie pushed Ida back toward Drew. He took her hand and towed her behind him through the house. The party was in full swing, and tons of the Bates family and friends were present. Ida saw Gracie's mom and waved to her in passing.

"Mom!" Drew called out.

Ida could feel Gracie behind her. Her giggles were a dead giveaway. They entered the kitchen, where Molly was taking a turkey out of the roaster and setting it down on a large platter.

Drew pulled her in front of him and wrapped his arms around her waist.

"Mom, I told you I was bringing my girlfriend—

He was cut off by Molly's scream. Her face split into a wide grin that reminded Ida so much of Drew. She rushed around the island and crushed her and Drew into a hard hug.

"I can't believe it!" Molly shouted. If she squeezed any harder, she was going to take the breath from Ida, who was smiling just as hard as his mother was. "I had always wished you two would get together. You make a handsome couple."

"Wait, what?" Drew laughed.

Molly stepped back and wiped her tears of joy away. She laughed and motioned to the two of them.

"Yes, I'll admit it. Ever since I met Ida, I knew she would be perfect for you," Molly said.

"And you didn't think to tell me?" Drew snorted. He wrapped his arms around Ida. She smiled and leaned into him. She felt warm and in love. She would have to find the perfect opportunity to tell him. Even though their relationship was swift, she didn't care. One thing she knew was that she didn't want to waste any more time. Drew was who she wanted to be with.

"Just like your brother, I knew you would eventually figure it out," Molly said. Ida glanced over and found Gracie with Harris. The two of them were perfect together. "Now, you kids get out of here. I have a few more things to do, then we can eat."

"YOUR MOTHER CAN COOK HER BUTT OFF," Ida groaned. Each year she came hungry but left stuffed when she attended the Bates family's Christmas Eve party. She carried her pile of dishes and followed Drew into the kitchen. They had volunteered to be part of the cleanup crew to help Mrs. Bates out. Harris and Gracie would be helping. They were organizing everything else that was left in the dining room.

The night had flown by. Ida didn't know

why she had been worried about what everyone would think. She had smiled and laughed the whole night. Luna had a fun night as well. Some of Drew's cousins who had children around her age had stopped by. Luna now had a few more friends to look forward to when she came to the party.

They placed their dishes on the counter, and Ida moved to the sink. She glanced around and didn't see any dish detergent. She refused to put some things in a dishwasher and wouldn't mind washing them by hand.

"Is your mom out of dish detergent?" she asked.

"Um, check the pantry over there. It should be on the bottom shelf." Drew pointed to the door in the corner of the room. She walked over to it and went into the pantry. She loved the Bates' home. Across from the pantry was a small coffee station that was cute and held everything one would need. A single pod coffee maker, a small fridge, a mug tree filled with matching porcelain mugs, and everything else required to doctor your drink.

Ida slipped inside the pantry and found

the detergent. She tried to walk back into the kitchen but Drew blocked her path.

"What are you doing?" she giggled. His grin widened as he pointed above them. She followed his hand and paused.

Mistletoe.

"Well, look at this," Drew murmured. He gathered her to him and cupped her cheeks. She leaned into his hold, returning his smile. "Ida, I know this past week has been a whirlwind, but there is one thing I know."

Her smile disappeared. Her heart pounded away. What was Drew about to say? Did he want to slow down their relationship? Take a step back? They had moved from zero to sixty quite fast.

"What is it, Drew?" she asked softly. Her breath hitched in her throat as she waited to hear what he had to say. She clutched the bottle of dish detergent to her chest.

"I love you."

Ida reached up and rested her hand along his. The joy inside of her exploded. These were words she had longed to hear but didn't think would happen so soon.

"I love you, too," she whispered. She

reached up and pulled him down to her, unable to wait any longer. He covered her mouth with his in a deep passionate kiss. She poured every ounce of love for this man into the kiss.

This week was turning into the best Christmas ever. Everyone had a wish this Christmas, and she had hers. She wished to spend the rest of her life with the man she loved.

EPILOGUE

"It's about time you were ready," Drew grumbled. He came up behind Ida and wrapped his arms around her. She had taken her time getting dressed and applying her makeup. He met her gaze in the mirror of their master bathroom. Much had happened in the past year. After the Christmas party, they were engaged shortly afterward, then married a few months later.

He palmed her round stomach and kissed the side of her neck. He inhaled deeply, breathing in her scent. He loved this woman more than life itself. He had gained not only a wife but a daughter and soon another child. After a brief thought, Drew talked with Ida about adopting Luna. That little girl owned a portion of his heart. They had gone through the process, and her father hadn't put up a fight. He'd signed his rights away, and yesterday it was official.

Luna's last name was officially Bates.

"Well, if a certain someone would allow me to leave the bed," Ida replied haughtily.

"Now, why would I do that?" Drew grinned. There was something about seeing his naked, pregnant wife lying in bed next to him that had him unable to keep his hands off her.

She spun around in his arms and tilted her head back. He pressed her against the counter. His cock was already hard and wanting her.

"We are going to be late," she huffed. She leaned up on her toes and pressed a kiss to his chin. "Come. Your family will be waiting."

She patted him on the shoulder and escaped his hold. She skated around him and headed into the bedroom.

"I don't know why you're rushing. It's not like you can put your boots on by yourself," Drew chuckled. Ida spun around and narrowed her beautiful eyes on him. He shrugged and ignored the daggers. "Am I lying?"

"Okay. Can you help me, please?" She batted those big brown eyes at him, and he had to adjust his cock. This year's Christmas Eve dinner would be extremely long if he didn't get any relief soon. She sat down on the bed and held her feet out towards him.

"When are we telling her?" he asked. He had been dying to share the good news with Luna.

"Want to do it today? She'd asked if she could open a gift today." Ida smiled at him. Drew knelt by her and assisted her with her boots. There wasn't anything he wouldn't do for his woman. She and Luna were both the reason he breathed.

"Yes." He leaned forward and pressed a kiss to her lips before jumping up. He rushed from the room and ran down the stairs of their new home. They had found a plot of land and had built their home from the ground up here in Langdale. They had moved in about a month ago. It was their dream home, and had plenty of room to expand their family. "Luna, come here."

He arrived on the first floor and went into their living room, where their ten-foot-tall Christmas tree was. Ida had made their house a home. The living room was full of decorations, while the scent of the live tree set the mood for the holidays. She had gone above and beyond with the decorations. She'd even had him outside putting up an inflatable Santa Claus and reindeer in their yard.

Ida went into the room and went over to sit on the couch. Boots barking announced that he and Luna were on their way to join them. Drew reached for a think rectangle box that had been wrapped with a bow on it.

"You called me?" Luna flew into the room. She was a miniature image of her mother. She was dressed in a red sweater dress with a black bow on the side of it. Her hair was pulled up into a single ponytail.

"Come here." He moved over to the couch and patted the area between him and Ida. Luna rushed over and wiggled her way in between them. Boots settled on the floor as if he wanted to see what was happening. "Your mom said you wanted to open one gift today."

"I don't get to pick it out?" She had been eyeing the large box resting near the tree all week. Even though Santa hadn't come, that box was labeled from the two of them.

"Nope. This is the one we want you to open." He handed it to her. Drew had never been so nervous in his life. He was a vet who was used to performing surgeries on animals who were considered part of a family, and he never broke a sweat like he was now. Ida's met his gaze over Luna's head while she ripped open the paper. Her warm brown eyes caused him to relax a little.

"What is it?" Luna asked, holding the black box in her hand.

"Open it, silly," he said. He raked his fingers through his hair to try to hide his nervousness. Ida helped Luna open the gift box. She pulled out the official looking certificate. Luna silently read the words on the page. Her hand froze in place. She glanced up at him, tears brimming in her eyes. Ida bit her lip, but tears were already flowing down her face.

Drew felt like sand had been thrown in his face. His eyes burned as he met Luna's stare.

"My name is Luna Bates now?" she whispered. She blinked, and the slow flow of tears started.

"Yeah, babe. It's official. I've adopted you. You're my daughter," Drew rasped. His throat constricted. Luna flew into his arms, wrapping him up tight in a hug. He collapsed his arms around her and held her to him. Her petite frame shook from the sobs that wracked her. "Are you okay?"

Her cries finally quieted. Ida had moved closer and rubbed her back with him.

"Luna, talk to us," Ida urged.

Luna pulled back and twisted around to settle on his lap.

"I'm so happy. I've wanted to call you daddy but didn't know if I should have, but now you are my daddy."

"Yeah, pumpkin. I'm your dad and would be honored to have you call me that." Drew's vision blurred. He held his little girl to him while wrapping his other arm around his wife.

This was the best Christmas he could ever wish for.

Missed the first book in this series, download Harris and Gracie's story, The Christmas Secret now!

A NOTE FROM THE AUTHOR

Dear reader,

Thank you for taking the time to read The Christmas Wish. I think I'm falling in love with this little town of Langdale. So much so, I think I'm going to continue writing holiday novellas in this town.

I hope you enjoyed Drew and Ida's story. I loved putting their story down on paper. It was just too cute for me not to share with you.

Happy holidays,
    Peyton Banks

P.S. Don't forget to leave a review after reading! Please note that no review is too small.

THE CHRISTMAS SECRET

There's no place like home for the holidays...

When her best friend comes home for the holidays, there is something different about him. Gracie Logan had been best friends with Harris since they were in junior high. Growing up, he had been the popular guy in town who all the women swooned over.

And she had been stuck in the friend category forever.

Keeping her lips sealed about her crush, she decided to continue being the one thing he needed most—a friend.

Harris Bates was home for the holidays.

One look at Gracie and knew he could no longer fight what he had known for years.

She was the one for him.

Sparks began to fly, and they can't ignore the intense attraction between them. Will they act on what is brewing between them? One thing they both knew was that nothing will ever be the same again.

The Christmas Secret is a steamy, holiday BWWM romance. For readers who love sexy, friends to lovers romance, this is for you. This short novella is reserved for mature readers only.

Available now!

ABOUT THE AUTHOR

USA TODAY bestselling author, Peyton Banks, is the alter ego of a city girl who is a romantic at heart. Her mornings consist of coffee and daydreaming up the next steamy romance book ideas. She loves spinning romantic tales of hot alpha males and the women they love. Make sure you check her out!

Sign up for Peyton's Newsletter to find out the latest releases, giveaways and news! Click HERE to sign up!

Want to know the latest about Peyton Banks? Follow her online:

ALSO BY PEYTON BANKS

Current Free Short Story

Summer Escape

The Keith Brothers

Mr. Hotness

Mr. Arrogant

Blazing Eagle Ranch Series

Back in the Saddle

Knockin' the Boots

Roping a Cowboy

Country at Heart

Cowboy, Take Me Away

Special Weapons & Tactics Series

Dirty Tactics (Special Weapons & Tactics 1)

Dirty Ballistics (Special Weapons & Tactics 2)

Dirty Operations (Special Weapons & Tactics 3)

Dirty Alliance (Special Weapons & Tactics 4)

Dirty Justice (Special Weapons & Tactics 5)

Dirty Trust (Special Weapons & Tactics 6)

Dirty Secrets (Special Weapons & Tactics 7)

Trust & Honor Series (BWWM)

Dallas

Dalton

A Langdale Christmas

The Christmas Secret

The Christmas Wish

Interracial Romances (BWWM)

Pieces of Me

Hard Love

Retain Me

Silent Deception

African American Romance

Breaking The Rules

Mafia Romance Series

Unexpected Allies (The Tokhan Bratva 1)

Made in the USA
Monee, IL
09 December 2023